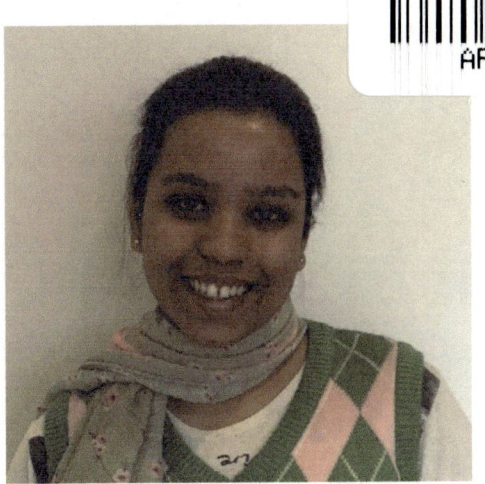

About the Author

Kareena Ghosh was born in 2009 in Coventry, UK, and moved to Australia in 2016. She loves reading and writing crime stories. When reading a crime novel, she likes to pit her wits against the protagonist or the detective and see if she can solve the crime before he or she can. In short, she would like to become an accomplished crime novel writer when she grows up. She entered a few literary competitions and won first prize in three poetry competitions and one short story competition. All her works have been published.

The Society of the Unwanted

Kareena Ghosh

The Society of the Unwanted

Olympia Publishers
London

www.olympiapublishers.com
OLYMPIA PAPERBACK EDITION

Copyright © Kareena Ghosh 2024

The right of Kareena Ghosh to be identified as author of
this work has been asserted in accordance with sections 77 and 78 of
the Copyright, Designs and Patents Act 1988.

All Rights Reserved

No reproduction, copy or transmission of this publication
may be made without written permission.
No paragraph of this publication may be reproduced,
copied or transmitted save with the written permission of the publisher,
or in accordance with the provisions
of the Copyright Act 1956 (as amended).

Any person who commits any unauthorised act in relation to
this publication may be liable to criminal
prosecution and civil claims for damage.

A CIP catalogue record for this title is
available from the British Library.

ISBN: 978-1-80439-598-1

This is a work of fiction.
Names, characters, places and incidents originate from the writer's
imagination. Any resemblance to actual persons, living or dead, is
purely coincidental.

First Published in 2024

Olympia Publishers
Tallis House
2 Tallis Street
London
EC4Y 0AB

Printed in Great Britain

Dedication

I dedicate this book to my parents who encouraged me to write this book.

Chapter 1

Harley was over cloud nine since an A-list magazine printed the detective story she wrote. From the tender age of six, Harley loved watching detective television shows and detective stories. Now that she turned twelve years old this year, she realised that the private eye must be in some way an unforgettable and remarkable character. He or she must be shrewd and judicious, of course, unusually intelligent, and perceptive, but also idiosyncratic, possessing perhaps some odd eccentricities that distinguished him or her.

Harley absolutely adored Nancy Drew books and loved her space-age gizmos and hybrid electric vehicle. She observed James Bond's groovy and high-tech gadgets, Columbo's crumpled raincoat and Kojak's lollipop; all these things made the hero somehow conspicuous. She was a courageous, confident, and adventurous girl; not much scared her.

Harley's detective character in her story was fifteen-year-old Lizzy McAdams, who wore a baggy granny dress and dark sunglasses. She was a witty and quirky Australian girl who spoke with a fake British accent. Her distinctive sunglasses were her secret tool that she used to deceive her opponents. Harley was dying to tell her friends the next day all about her story publication.

She had been friends with Melissa, Adam, and Kai since pre-school. They shared a deep and sweet friendship that refreshed the soul. It was very coincidental that they were all born on the same date and celebrated their birthdays together. They were all twelve-year-olds who studied at the prestigious Pembroke Royal Academy.

Situated in a leafy suburb of Sydney, Pembroke Royal Academy was officially one of Australia's strictest schools. The school's stringent rules and record-breaking results made it so appealing to parents in Sydney and the surrounding suburbs that there were about sixty thousand applications for fifty places in the school every year. Some parts of the school building, though fairly new, were built in Elizabethan style. The main entry was the most ostentatious and elaborate part of the school building – a curious mix of heraldic pretension and classical columns, profuse carvings, and ornate decorations. The hallways had dark marble floors and white walls, not a handprint or scuff mark anywhere.

It was lunchtime at the school, but the children did not get a chance to eat much. Their plates of fries and a chicken patty were just about half-eaten when a dinner warden swiftly removed them. The children sitting on either side passed their plates to the end in pin-drop silence.

Since the entire school had first sat down to have lunch, it had only been ten minutes. On the adjacent tables, other adult guests dashed to finish their meals in the challenge of stretched-out hands attempting to take their plates, as teachers in ineffable moods gauged the students' progress. At this school, 'family meals' aimed to foster soft skills; children were not expected to converse, but were encouraged to pour drinks, and clear plates – whether they had finished their meal or not.

Mr Tony Westman, the principal or 'headmaster', who founded Pembroke Royal Academy ten years ago, said the school's emphasis on orderliness and discipline meant that 'kids could be kids there, and have real upbringings'. The approach was intended to remove space for the social ills that other schools grapple with – Mr Westman said the hushed corridors almost eradicated bullying, though he agreed that online bullying was harder to eliminate. The school days were run with military meticulousness.

Everything was scheduled to the second, from lessons to meals, with the help of gigantic digital clocks in each room. Before counting down backwards, teachers would often give their students a time limit to complete a task: "Twelve seconds to take out your books and turn to page one hundred and twenty-six."

The classrooms were designed to incorporate end-user requirements, environmental factors, material, equipment, technology requirements, and health and safety considerations. The doors were a glossy black, numbered with silver digits to notify the classroom year and section, which also matched the globe shaped handles.

The science laboratory incorporated a range of features, including a remodelled horseshoe desk layout, which allowed space for the teacher to circulate freely and easily, reducing the lines of communication and also helping the teachers to keep an eye on the students' progress. Power modules were built in the student desks for easy accessibility and a teacher wall complete with a whiteboard, interactive screen, and in-built storage to minimise clutter.

The transition between classes was carefully timed and done in complete silence. A line of blue lights ran down the middle of the pristine dark marble corridors, and the youngsters were expected to go silently down either side to their next classes, almost like ghosts. Teachers with keen eyes were on the lookout for students who were walking too slowly. Every aspect was designed to help you get the most out of your study time. There were no mirrors in the student restrooms because they would divert the students' attention.

It was always clear to Harley that she and her three friends were a lot more different than all the other kids in her school. Firstly, they had a unique perspective on things. They always saw ridiculously intricate details in even simple situations. Secondly, they possessed curiosity coupled with an exceptional understanding of the rules of evidence, the ability to talk to people and elicit information from them, and a lot of patience. Also, they were not willing to accept things at face value and dig deep into why something happened.

They were the detectives of their school until Mr Westman banned them from their detective business.

"Look, you are all very good kids but the next time you do this sort of spying around, the consequence might be expulsion," Mr Westman said sternly. He also gave a plethora of reasons why spying is not for kids. The four youngsters argued with the principal until they had to give up due to his steely, hard-nosed, and unrelenting attitude.

Chapter 2

The children were miserable for a month until each of them got a knock at the door of their houses at four a.m.

When the teenagers opened their respective doors, questioning who would arrive at someone's house that early in the morning, they found a man with a soot-black mask on who gave them a glass bottle with a message inside, ran to a white van, and then drove away. This was very unbelievable for all of them except Kai, who expected it to be a letter to become a ninja, already knowing he was going to be a ninja when he grew up.

"Finally, this took so long to get here. I knew I could be a ninja. I would be so good at being one!" Kai exclaimed happily.

It was overly complex to open the bottle to get to the note. Harley threw the glass bottle at her brick wall; Kai used a glass cutter, and Adam just jumped on his bottle. Since Melissa was quite strong already, she opened it perfectly without breaking the glass. After they got out the note, they all read the notes that they had gotten.

All the notes said, 'Come to 24 Cunnington Street at seven a.m. tomorrow' and, at the very bottom of the note, it said, 'TELL NO ONE'. Tomorrow was the start of the weekend, and all the kids were disappointed that the appointment was so early in the morning.

Kai was saddened that it was not the ninja school

acceptance letter.

This could be a new mystery. I think I should check it out, Adam thought to himself. Adam packed all the spy equipment he got for his birthday last year and was happy that he could finally use it for an actual mystery. The next day, each of the teenagers came out of their houses to find out why they all got this bizarre and puzzling letter. It was a very strange location to meet at because 24 Cunnington Street was the abandoned science lab that everyone in their suburb had forgotten about, and no one had ever been in there since the nuclear incident ten years ago.

When they arrived, they were shocked that their friends were there too. "What are you all doing here?" they exclaimed simultaneously.

"Okay, why are you guys here too? Did you get a bottle just like me?" Docile Melissa asked in her dulcet tone.

"You all got a bottle because I need you all," a shady, tall, and slim figure said nonchalantly.

"Who are you, and what do you want from us?" Harley asked.

"I am William the Wizard, and I know something that none of you know about yourselves. You can leave if you want, or you can stay and I will tell you what I know," William said.

Intrigued by the situation, the kids decided to stay.

"I see you all decided to stay. Every one of you has one magical power that would be extremely useful, but they have not been activated yet," William exclaimed.

"Why should we believe you if we don't even know you?" Melissa asked.

William took out an apple from his pocket and after a

few seconds, the apple started levitating. The kids were amazed to find out that magic was real.

"How do we even activate our powers then?" Kai asked.

"You need to hold hands and say, 'Me oh my, please get me by and bring my powers to me'," William the Wizard elucidated.

The four kids all did what he said, and an emerald-green light appeared around them, and each of their cheeks glowed with rainbow colours. "Wow! How did you know we even had powers in the first place?" Harley asked.

"You all were born on 15 March 2009 in the local hospital. I knew I needed a few people to protect our world, and I was in such a rush to find humans who could help in my situation. I went to the nearest place I could find, that was the hospital. I had a potion which gave any human powers to become very mighty and powerful. I remember that the potion in my bag did not have the cap on because it popped off the bottle a few minutes before while I was running into the hospital. So, it spilled on the only four babies in the hospital. That is you four. My goblin friend made the potion with this magical chemical named Moralesium, which, if any living creature except goblins and humans touch, then they would all turn into ash, so I could not touch the potion. Hence, I could not clean it up," William clarified.

"Why did you get us to activate our powers?" Adam asked.

"I need your help to find the missing people in this city, and I want you to track down the source of them. Just remember not to tell anyone because it could risk your safety," William said, mystified.

"A new mystery!" Melissa said happily.

The teenagers went back to their homes, thrilled that they would be able to be back in action and become true detectives now for a real crime, but, on top of all that, they had powers now too! Harley was so happy that she could now be a living Lizzy McAdams and wrote all about it in her newest Lizzy story, except instead of using her own name, she wrote Lizzy's name. She sometimes talked to Lizzy when she was alone because she was an only child and had no siblings to ask for advice and thought of her as a real friend and even a real sister.

"Lizzy, I had the most tremendous day! I just found out that I actually have powers. Can you believe that I'm just like you now?" she said boldly. Just one second after Harley finished her conversation with Lizzy, Harley's mum came barging into the room and told her dinner was ready. Harley went and ate, fantasising about her life as a superhero spy detective.

Adam was practising for his spelling bee coming up, trying to clear his head from what he had just found out a few hours ago. He had such mixed feelings about this. He did not have anyone to talk to except his older sister, who was in university, and his parents worked full-time jobs. He had lots of spare time on his hands, which he spent thinking about various things. His only other option, which was investigating with his friends, was taken away by Mr Westman. Adam was a very straightforward person. As he was practising for his spelling competition, he thought about all the information William the Wizard gave them today. His brain was a bit scrambled, but at the same time, he was super excited at the prospect of solving new mysteries with his friends.

He was not going to investigate petty things anymore. He was worried about bad people and villains trying to attack him, but he was excited to start being a detective with his friends again. He always thought that wizards were a myth, but since he had just met one, he was thinking about what other mythical creatures were in our universe. After he practised for his spelling bee, he watched a few fantasy movies on his monitor to discover what people did when they found out they had powers. All night after that, he wondered how getting these powers would affect his life.

As soon as he got home, Kai tried to use his powers, not knowing what they were or how they worked, but he got bored easily. So, after twenty minutes, he went to play ping pong with his brother Kija and forgot all about the powers he had just discovered he had. He always forgot about everything while playing sports with his brother, and it gave him time to bond with him. "Did anything happen to you because you sneaked out pretty early this morning for a long time?" his brother Kija asked curiously. Kai just remembered what had happened and froze. He missed the ping pong ball that was flying towards him, and it hit his forehead.

"Are you okay? You just missed when I hit to you, and you usually never miss. Anyway, let's just keep on going," Kai's brother questioned, concerned.

They stopped communicating for a while until they had a break for a few minutes.

"You are acting really extraordinarily strange today," Kija said, chuckling.

"Of course, I'm fine. Why wouldn't I be? It was just an average regular day. I went out to go to the mall," Kai answered wearily, feeling guilty for lying to his brother.

"Really? You hate the mall. Whenever mum asks us if we want to go shopping, you remind her each time that you despise malls," Kija replied.

Out of all places in this town, I choose the mall. Great, now I must dig deeper into this lie, Kai thought.

"Well, I changed my mind. Is changing your mind a crime now?" Kai responded. Kija was confused about how Kai was acting, but he just ignored it, and the two brothers went back and played ping-pong for the rest of the day.

Melissa went home to her family. She had a younger sister and brother who were fraternal twins, one baby sister, one older brother, and one older sister. When she got home, Melissa found her older sister, Nicole, sitting on the couch talking to her friend on the phone.

"Where is Dad?" Melissa asked.

"He went to work at the restaurant," Nicole replied, looking agitated. Melissa's family owned a restaurant called Dimitriou's Diner, as her family's last name is Dimitriou. She never saw her parents anymore, ever since they built the diner. It was a Greek restaurant, given that Melissa's mum and dad were both born in Greece.

Her mum said that Melissa's grandmother taught her every recipe she knew. The restaurant served popular Greek dishes, including mezethes, moussaka, baklava, souvlaki, fasolakia lathera, and many more. It was quite busy and noisy most of the time as Greeks are known to enjoy their food and spend hours after their meal talking and having a great time.

Melissa walked to her room, slumping a bit because of the rough and tiring day she had had. She bumped into her little sister Rhea, who was running away from her twin brother Jonas. "Stop running in the house, you two. You could get hurt!" Melissa told them. They slowed down after she warned them, and Melissa went into her room and shut the door behind her. She had a lot of trophies squished onto a shelf in her bedroom because she took part in tennis competitions. She had won every one of the competitions that she participated in in the last four years. Melissa flopped onto her bed and sighed.

"This is so exciting; I wonder what magic I have. I really want to rub it in Nicole's face that I have powers and she does not, so she can stop being so bossy and rude to me. Then she will really want to hang out with me, but that William the Wizard man said I cannot tell anyone," Melissa said to herself.

After a few minutes, Melissa's mum barged into her room with her baby sister Selene in her arm.

"Honey, it is time for your tennis practise in fifteen minutes. Get dressed," her mum said kindly to her.

"Mum, I am really tired today; can I practise tomorrow?" Melissa asked in a wobbly voice.

"Then you shouldn't have gone out today so early in the morning. Plus, it's only three-fifteen p.m. right now, so you can't be that tired. We spend money for your lessons with Laine, and you need to appreciate that more. We do this for you to follow you dream and become a professional tennis star, so you are going, no excuses," Melissa's mum replied and shut the door.

Melissa groaned and then put on her tennis clothes. For

the rest of the day, Melissa played tennis with her instructor, Laine.

The next day, Harley sent out a text to all her friends as soon as she woke up, asking if they could meet up today at Living the Ice Cream, which was an ice cream shop opposite Harley's house. They all agreed to meet up at two-thirty p.m. Harley brought a notepad in case any of her friends had a thought about where the missing people were. The first to arrive was Melissa, who looked very tired while coming in.

"What happened to you?" Harley asked her.

"I had to work at the restaurant all day before I could come here. For some reason, there were more customers than usual. Most of them were men in the same black T-shirts," Melissa replied.

"That is really weird. Maybe men who like wearing black like Greek food?" Harley wondered, drawing a man in a black T-shirt like Melissa described in her notepad. A few minutes later, Adam came walking through the door.

"Hey, Harley. Hey, Melissa. Sorry I'm late. I forgot that we were meeting. Before my mum left for work, she said I had to finish my homework prior to going out anywhere," Adam elucidated.

"That is okay, Adam, Kai hasn't even come yet. We were just talking about school while we were waiting for you to get here," Melissa said. Kai came after four minutes, and he was totally out of breath.

"I am so sorry, my dear friends. I was playing board games with my family, also surfing the web on my phone. Then I looked at your texts, but I had to stay for the rest of the game, but as soon as it ended, I came running over here," Kai said amazingly fast. He fell back into a chair and sighed.

"Okay, since we are all here, we have to talk about our powers and about who has taken all the people who have gone missing," Harley whispered.

"William said we all have individual powers. What do you think they are?" Adam questioned.

"I hope I can read minds!" Melissa said excitedly.

"Wait, before we talk about all of this, we need to order some ice cream, or this shop will kick us out of here," Kai said.

They all ordered one ice cream each. Harley got cookies and cream, Adam got chocolate, Kai got pistachio, and Melissa got vanilla. After they got their ice creams, they sat down at the table they were sitting at before and started talking about their powers.

"I really want to fly. I could zoom around the town whenever I wanted, and I could spend time together with birds. Or maybe I could have super strength, then I could lift anything I want, and I could defeat bad guys easily when I become a ninja," Kai said.

"Well, I want to talk to animals, so when I become a vet, it will be easy for me to find out what's wrong with everyone's pets!" said Adam.

"I haven't really given it much thought, but I would like to have invisibility," said Harley.

A few minutes later, a man that looked exactly like how Melissa described came into the ice cream shop. Melissa gave Harley a nudge and pointed to the man.

"That looks exactly like the man that you described," Harley whispered. "I wonder what all these men are doing at these shops," Melissa said.

She looked out of the window and saw that two other men in black T-shirts with shopping bags in their hands were coming out of a Chinese restaurant right next to Living the Ice Cream. They got into a black car and waited inside for a long time. Melissa asked Harley if they should go follow them, and since Harley liked investigating a lot, she agreed. They confided in Kai and Adam about the men, and Harley showed them her drawing.

They both thought it was weird, but Adam suggested it could be just a coincidence. They all must just be hungry and trying out restaurants of their liking. After Melissa and Harley explained the situation a bit more, they agreed to go and follow them. Thankfully, the black car hadn't left yet. They waited until the man in the ice cream shop left and got in the car. The car drove off really fast, making a screeching sound. The children tried to run after the car, but they all got tired very quickly and gave up.

After a little while, the four friends walked back to Adam's house to find out more about the source. Adam was excellent at coding and hacking. They agreed to find more about the source and find out how many people went missing.

For a few hours, they were digging up things on the internet and all the news about the missing people. They also read about the missing people reports. The missing people consisted of twelve kids and fourteen adults. While they were reading, they heard shattered glass and turned around. Eight large men with masks surrounded them.

The kids were terrified, but a second later, they found themselves outside their school. They did not understand what happened and how they got to the school, but Kai's palm had a light inside of it.

"I think teleportation is your magical power, Kai!" Harley exclaimed.

"Wow, that really saved us, but how are we going to get back? Do we even know if those guys are still there?" Kai asked.

"How about you teleport us to the shed in my backyard? There is a clear view of the window of my bedroom, and we can see if they are still there," Adam answered.

"I don't even know how I did that," Kai replied.

"Did you think of school when we were in Adam's bedroom?" Harley asked.

"No, I just wished we were somewhere safe," Kai answered.

"Well, school is a very safe place. Please wish that you were in my backyard," Adam asked.

Kai did what Adam told him to do, and the group all landed in the shed in his backyard.

They could see no one in Adam's bedroom, so the group came out of the shed and went back upstairs. "Do you think that the guys who broke in are working for the person who took the missing people?" Melissa asked.

"Yes, I think they might have found out we were uncovering information about the missing people and tracked our location," Adam stated.

The gang thought about the men they saw burst through the window until, out of nowhere, Melissa morphed into one of the men. Like Kai, she had a light inside of her palm.

"Oh my gosh, what happened? Why do my fingers look so swollen up?" Melissa cried.

Her friends looked at her in awe. "Wow, your power is shape shifting!" Adam said excitedly.

"That's great, but I don't want to look like this forever. How do I switch back?" Melissa asked worriedly.

"Kai thought of where he wanted to go, so maybe you should think of yourself," Adam suggested.

Then a few seconds later, she changed back to her normal self. "Thank goodness that I didn't have to look like that for the rest of my life," Melissa said, relieved.

"I wouldn't want my best friend to be a big, thirty-year-old man for the rest of my life," Harley laughed.

"At least two of us know what our powers are now and how we can control them," Kai said.

The gang slept over at Kai's house that night, as they were very paranoid and afraid of the men who had just broken into Adam's house a few hours ago. Adam's parents brought in a window repair man to fix the smashed window. They had no choice but to lie that they broke the window while playing basketball in the backyard.

"I hope that those guys don't break into my house this time," Kai said.

"They only broke into my house because they knew about us looking through the files of the missing people," Adam explained.

"I'm honestly glad that I can finally get a good rest without so much noise coming from downstairs," Melissa sighed in relief.

"My parents are going to dinner at this fancy restaurant, so you won't have to hear my dad's snoring," Kai exclaimed.

Everyone started to drift off to sleep, except for Harley,

who was thinking of how terrifying it would be if the men who broke into Adam's house would have captured them and what they might have done if they got kidnapped like the missing people. Harley got up to go to the bathroom when Kai's parents just got back from their dinner. "Hello, Mr and Mrs Lee, how was your dinner?" Harley asked.

"To be honest, Harley, it didn't go so well as we planned it to be," Mrs Lee sighed.

"The restaurant was full, so we had to eat at this fast-food truck because it was the only other place providing food in that area. It was very strange, all the people who were at the restaurant were wearing the same clothes," Mr Lee explained.

"What were the people wearing?" Harley asked.

"Everyone was wearing a black shirt with black jeans, and they all were men. Maybe they are theatre actors wearing the same clothes," Mrs Lee said.

Harley's eyes became very wide, and she was nearly about to scream, but she just went back into Kai's bedroom and tried to wake everyone. She told them all about what Kai's parents just told her.

Kai pointed out that there is no point going back to the restaurant as the guys in the black attires might have left by now. But instead, they could go back to Adam's room to look for evidence.

"Maybe we should look for any clues or DNA samples the bad guys left behind in Adam's room," Kai said.

They teleported themselves to Adam's room with Kai's special power. They searched and searched until Melissa found a single hair strand on Adam's bed.

"Guys, I found something!" Melissa exclaimed,

holding up the hair strand.

"It could just be mine, but we can look anyway," Adam said.

Like a whiz kid, Adam quickly analysed the DNA sample. He found it belonged to a man named 'Jack Raines' who works at Mac's Lamps, a store that sells lamps a block away from his house. The group decided to go to Mac's Lamps to find out more.

When they finally arrived, they saw that it was empty, so they went inside and looked for hints. They looked everywhere, but Kai somehow accidentally knocked over an old and dusty lamp. Under the lamp, there was a bright red button.

Kai was tempted by the red button, so he pressed it, and it opened a secret passageway that was blocked by shelves of lamps. The group was amazed, and out of curiosity, they went inside. Once inside, they found a man with a dark cloak, staring at a large group of people. They were kneeling with masks over their eyes and mouths. Their hands and feet were tied. He turned around to find the four children in his secret room.

"Who are you and what are you doing?" Harley asked.

"I am the King of Greed, and this is my army," he said, pointing to the people with blindfolds on. He walked towards the group and said, "I think I found four more members to join my brigade. The memory washing will be in a few minutes."

The group was really shocked about what the King of Greed just stated. He said that he would brainwash them and the people who were held captive so that he could make them worship him and do whatever he told them to do. Just after the King of Greed spoke, the same eight men who came to Adam's house appeared behind them. They had nowhere to run, so they accepted their fate until each of the teenagers' cheeks started glowing again, just like they did when they activated their powers. In each of the kids' hands, glowing orbs appeared that were as hot as lava.

After a few seconds, the orbs levitated, and the whole room glowed up with iridescent and lucent lights from the orbs. The King of Greed covered his eyes as the lights dazzled his vision, and then all the orbs hit the King of Greed. His cloak fell onto the ground, and when Kai picked it up, there was nothing under it. Intoxicating earth aromas induced lassitude and ethereal calm in the atmosphere. Totally shocked, the eight men ran away, shrieking because they saw what just happened to the King of Greed.

Adam noticed them running away and chased after them. Melissa, Harley, and Kai untied the people with blindfolds. The captives' emotions changed from angst to joyful epiphany. They were euphoric that they were free. They thanked the children immensely and left for their home.

When Adam came back, he explained that he found a police officer on the side of the road and told him about the eight men. Then the police officer started running after them to catch the criminals, who surrendered without much fight. They were all happy that everyone was safe and that they did not get their memories wiped out.

The four friends went back to Adam's house after that and celebrated together that they had stopped the King of Greed. After a few hours of celebrating, the teenagers heard a knock on the door. Adam went to open the door and found that William the Wizard was standing at the door, so he called everyone to see him.

"How did you know where we were?" Harley asked.

"I know where each of you live, and that is how I brought the bottles to you. I saw on the news that the nefarious villains who captured the missing people have been arrested, and I knew that I should congratulate you and come to each of your houses, but since you are all already here, I wanted to say thank you for all your challenging work. I also wanted to ask you something," William explained.

He continued, "I want you four to be my new team of wizards and learn more about your powers and also stop people who try to destroy the world."

"Of course, we would love to learn more about our powers, and we can become real detectives now!" Kai exclaimed.

"I have thought about the perfect name we can call ourselves, The Society of the Unwanted!" Melissa said excitedly. Since that day, the four friends have been known as the Society of the Unwanted and have saved lives every day since then.

Chapter 3

It was almost Christmas; the summer holidays had started. Though the children were excited about Christmas, things were getting monotonous. They were getting bored; it had been incredibly quiet for almost two weeks. Their new 'office' was in Kai's treehouse with a sign that read, "The Society of the Unwanted." Kai's dog, CeCe, was inducted as their sidekick, similar to Scooby-Doo assisting Shaggy in solving crimes. William the Wizard had disappeared from the scene for nearly two weeks. The children yearned to find an intriguing new mystery that they could solve.

In the meantime, Harley had been reading all types of crime stories, from suspenseful thrillers to amusing mysteries, snug whodunits to hard-edged detective stories, set in a variety of places from fast-paced New York to turn of the century Prague to both Victorian and modern-day England, and written by the different leading or little-known authors. She met with her friends every day in the evening to tell all about the crime stories she had been reading.

It was a Tuesday when Harley heard a knock at her door. It was William the Wizard. He said, "Harley, something particularly important has come up. We need to convene a meeting immediately. Could you please get hold of the other children?" Harley nodded and phoned Kai, Melissa, and Adam and asked them to meet at the treehouse in fifteen minutes.

Everyone gathered at the tree house. William the Wizard told them, "I have been contacted by the coastguard regarding stolen ancient artefacts from Egypt that have been smuggled into Australia. A few consignments have already arrived in Sydney, but we do not know where they are being stored. We need to locate these expensive artefacts and return them to Egypt. I need your help guys. Once I know more, I will come Friday and meet you at the same time as today. If you hear or see something unusual, let me know immediately."

He left, and the children were baffled by the information or the lack of it. They did not know where to start but decided to walk around in different coastal suburbs of Sydney to see if they could spot something unusual. They returned home tired and empty-handed.

That night, Kai was woken up by CeCe's savage barking. He was worried that a thief must be lurking around his house, waiting to break in.

Kai shouted, "What's up, boy, did you hear something in there?" CeCe was standing in front of the closet door right beside the large floor-to-ceiling window and growling. "Do not worry, perhaps it is just a cat or a mouse; let's go back to sleep."

In fact, he could have sworn it sounded kind of like a giggle and thought, *Do cats or mice giggle?* He decided to clear out his wardrobe to figure out what was going on and find the underlying cause of this mystery but did not find anything. Scanning through the room again, he could not find anything. His parents knew about the rattling sounds in Kai's bedroom and marked it up to a boy's wild imagination. Kai made a 'friendly' mousetrap out of a bolstered empty cereal box with cheese and peanut butter on a paper plate.

It was almost midnight; he looked out through his bedroom window and was surprised that there was a large removal truck parked outside their late neighbour's house. Kai's neighbour across the street, Mrs Higgins, had passed away two months ago. She was an old lady who lived alone and had no relatives except a granddaughter who lived in Paris, who visited her once a year during Christmas.

Kai's mum, Kwan, took it upon herself to look after Mrs Higgins. She cooked her Sunday dinner and took it over to her house and, sometimes, even drove her to her doctor's appointments. Kwan was really saddened by Mrs Higgins' demise and organised a small remembrance ceremony for her.

Kai was intrigued why someone would be moving into Mrs Higgins' house in the middle of the night. He thought maybe Mrs Higgins' granddaughter decided to leave her job in Paris and move back to Sydney.

After half an hour, the removal truck was gone, and all the lights in Mrs Higgins house were switched off. The next morning at breakfast, Kai told them what he saw. Kwan was really surprised that Mrs Higgins' granddaughter, Angelica, would move from Paris to Sydney as she was the CEO of a top financial company, La Banque Postale. She said that she would give her a few days to settle and then visit her to say hello.

The children walked around the neighbourhood on Wednesday and decided that it was not a wise way to look for smugglers. It was impossible to say whether a truck was stashed with priceless antiquities from another country without breaking into it.

On Wednesday night, Kai was awoken by the noise of the cereal box falling to the floor: there stood a white furry round-bodied mouse. Peanut butter smudged all over his face, clutching a tiny piece of cheese in his petite hands. Kai asked, "How come you did not get trapped? You surely are one lucky little fella." The mouse chuckled, twitched his nose, and scurried away.

Kai looked at his bedroom window and the night sky was aglow with bright lights. He peeped through the window, and there was the removal truck again outside Mrs Higgins' house. The removal guys were unloading long and heavy objects in the house. It looked like all four removalists were men. Again, like the night before, they left in a hurry.

Kai informed the gang about what he had seen the past two nights. He had a hunch that there was something fishy happening at his neighbour's house. It is not coincidental that the removalist would deliver at night-time, two nights in a row.

Harley said, "I wish William the Wizard was here to tell us what to do. But I do not want to disturb him if the removalists are genuine and not bad people."

The children decided to have a stakeout in Kai's treehouse that night because they would have a better view of the removalists if they came to deliver again.

Kai asked Kwan, "Hey, Mom, where did you keep my Mickey Mouse sleeping bag?" His mom was in the kitchen baking chocolate cupcakes with Kija and his little sister, Ki. Kija totally ignored him as he was busy licking the chocolate spoon.

Kwan said, "On your top shelf of your closet, dear; remember you put it there after your school camp last summer?"

He asked if she would get it down for him. "Sorry, I have the cupcakes in the oven right now. If you get the small ladder, you should be able to reach it yourself." Kai realised his mom was right; he was able to grab the bag. He tossed the bag out into the room as he jumped down from the ladder and a brilliant idea crossed his mind.

He pretended to be famished and asked Kwan to give him a cupcake. The cupcake was really delicious. Kai asked Kwan if she had a few spare cupcakes. Kwan said that she had baked quite a few cupcakes as she wanted to take a few to the homeless shelter.

Kai suggested his mum take a few cupcakes over to Mrs Higgins' house and say hello to Angelica. Kwan thought that was a great idea and quickly packed ten cupcakes in a plastic container. She walked over to Mrs Higgins' house and knocked on the door. Surprisingly, Mr Bond answered the door. Mr Bond's house was right beside Mrs Higgins' house. He looked uncomfortable and sheepish.

Kwan apologised for disturbing him. She told him that she expected that Angelica had returned from Paris, and that was the reason she brought some cupcakes for her. Mr Bond seemed to have composed himself and told Kwan that Angelica would be returning to Sydney at the beginning of next year. She had already sent some of her furniture from Paris and asked him to receive them in the house.

Kwan did not want Mr Bond to think she was rude and handed him the cupcakes. She returned to her house feeling a bit hurt that Angelica did not trust her to receive the furniture at her house.

Mr Bond was a lonely, sketchy character in his mid-forties and never interacted with any of the neighbours. Mrs Higgins and Kwan discussed many a time how unsocial Mr Bond was. He never made any eye contact and had a few shady looking characters hanging around his house. Kwan could not understand why Angelica would entrust Mr Bond with her house keys.

Kwan came back to the house with a bruised ego and told her family what happened at Mrs Higgins' house. Kai was suspicious but was not fully convinced that spying on Mrs Higgins' house would achieve anything. Maybe Mr Bond was telling the truth and he was just being good and helpful neighbour who was there to lend a hand. Kai updated the other children about his mom's visit, but they decided to go ahead with the night watch at his neighbour's house. If they achieve nothing from this night watch, at least they would have a fun night with their friends.

Adam, Harley, and Melissa joined Kai for the treehouse night watch. Everything was ready; the sleeping bags were laid out, along with a flashlight, his Laser Blaster, and packets of crisps and cookies.

Kai's dad shouted from the bottom of the tree. "Son, are you in here? Bring your friends with you. Dinner has already been served."

The friends' heads popped up from the gate of the treehouse. Kai screamed back, "Okay Dad, we are coming down."

Eating as fast as they could, they jumped up from the table. "What's the rush?" his mom asked. "I made your favourite raspberry pecan crust pie."

The tangy smell of raspberry and toasted pecan nuts left Adam drooling, but Kai said, "No time for pie; got to get ready for our camp-out. Can we be excused, please?"

"All right but take four pieces of pie with you," Mum retorted.

Ki whined, "Hey, that is not fair; I want to camp too!"

Rushing to the kitchen for their pie pieces, Kai yelled, "Well, you are not camping with us!"

Ki started to cry; after all, she was only three and a half. Kwan picked Ki up and told her that she could camp in her room with her Barbie dolls. Ki was overly excited, wriggled out of Kwan's arms, and ran to her room to gather all her Barbie dolls.

At the tree house, the children started playing different board games like Monopoly, Scrabble and even played Roblox on their iPads. At eleven forty-five p.m., they decided just to switch off the lights and wait for the removal van to arrive. At exactly five minutes past midnight, the removal van arrived. Four men jumped out of the van. One of them knocked on the door, and Mr Bond came out.

Kai told the other children, "This is highly suspicious, guys. Why would Mr Bond want to receive items in the middle of the night at Mrs Higgins' house? We need to investigate this."

Melissa said, "You are right. We should wait till these guys leave. I hope Mr Bond will go back to his own house after the delivery and then Kai can teleport himself to Mrs Higgins' house. You can open up one or two of the boxes to see what's inside."

Adam stated, "I have a better idea. I have realised that

my superpower is mind reading, but I need to be close enough to Mr Bond and look into his eyes to read his mind. Tomorrow morning, I will go to Mr Bond's house to sell cookies for fundraising and try to read his mind."

After the truck left, to the children's dismay, Mr Bond did not return to his house. They tried to stay awake as long as they could but went to sleep after an hour. They could not fathom why Mr Bond would not return to his own house if he was just receiving boxes and furniture for Angelica. Who gave him keys to the house? If Mr Bond did not speak to anybody in the neighbourhood, how did Angelica manage to contact him and ask him to receive her belongings?

The next morning, the children went back to their houses, freshened up, had their breakfast, and returned to Kai's tree house. They were waiting for William when they saw Mr Bond mowing his front lawn. He must have returned to his home early that morning. Adam quickly took out his cookies and arranged them on a tray. He ran to Mr Bond's lawn while Kai teleported himself to Mrs Higgins' house.

Adam asked Mr Bond whether he would like to buy some cookies for charity. He said rudely that he was not interested. Adam tried to strike a conversation with him and even volunteered to mow the rest of his lawn for a dollar.

Adam tried to read his mind, but the only thing Mr Bond was thinking was how to get rid of him. Adam had no other choice but to return to the treehouse. He could feel Mr Bond's eyes were fixated on him. Was he doubtful of his motive? Harley told Adam that he should have taken a detour and not have come directly to Kai's house as Mr

Bond was now suspicious of everyone in the house.

In the meantime, Kai teleported himself inside Mrs Higgins' house. There were about twenty wooden crates of assorted sizes stored all around the house. Kai tried to open one of the crates. It was packed so meticulously that it was difficult to get into. He teleported himself inside the largest crate that was four times as big as him. He switched on the torch, and inside he found a beautiful statue of an ancient soldier.

He was scared that he would be caught, so he quickly teleported himself back to the tree house. He informed everyone what he found inside the wooden crate. They were thrilled to bits as they knew they were about to solve a crime all by themselves.

William arrived shortly, and Harley briefed him about devious Mr Bond. William was overly excited about the new developments. He said that twenty Egyptian statues and rare masterpieces were stolen from a Cairo Museum. They had landed in Sydney, and a dodgy port worker allowed these pieces to be smuggled in without any hassle. The police caught the port worker after $50,000 was transferred to his bank account from Dubai. The bank became highly suspicious of this transfer as the port worker never had more than $100 in his account. They contacted the police, and after interrogation, the port worker confessed to allowing in the smuggled goods, but he did not know where these valuable pieces were currently stored.

William called 000, and the police came immediately. Mr Bond was arrested, and all the prized Egyptian pieces were retrieved. Mr Bond took advantage of Mrs Higgins' death and used her house to store the statues. As the boxes were quite large, he could not store them in his own house as it would be difficult to move around with large boxes in his house.

The Egyptian government was informed about the retrieval, and The Society of the Unwanted received medals and rare memorabilia. The Sydney police also gave them medals and allowed them to ride in a police van for four hours. Though the school was shut for the summer holidays, the school principal, Mr Westman, sent them a long email congratulating them for their bravery and astute detective work. He also added that he changed his mind about not allowing them to do any detective and investigative work in the school. The gang was overjoyed at the outcome, and William lauded them for their arduous work. He left, saying that he would be in touch soon with the new case.

Chapter 4

It was the second week since school started after the summer holidays. Harley and her friends were thrilled and excited to visit Canberra on a school excursion. Mr Westman was accompanying them on the trip. He asked everyone to gather near the clock tower at the Sydney Central railway station sharp at six forty-five a.m. the next day. At assembly, he made everyone streamline their watches to the school watch so that no one was late, even by a second. The train was leaving at 7.12 a.m. Apparently, the train running on the route was well-equipped, comfortable, and would take about four and a half hours from Sydney Central railway station to Canberra Kingston station.

They all boarded the train in an organised manner. The friends were sitting together, accompanied by their classmate Terence. Terence had been hanging around the detective friends since the school opened in the New Year. He made it clear that he wanted to be their assistant. Suddenly, an unusual looking man boarded the train at the last minute. He seemed to be out of breath. Terence had been noticing the man since the train left Sydney Central station. He had a huge shiny head, tan-coloured skin, thick lips, flat nose, and puffy cheeks. He had a horrible cut mark on the cheek. There was a hint of cruelty on his face.

It was cloudy and raining outside, but he had thick

green sunglasses glued to his eyes. Terence eyed him surreptitiously, noting the oddly showy silver watch chain peeking from his waistcoat pocket. Even in the heat of February, he was wearing a high neck full shirt with a grey waistcoat. The colour of the shirt was black with milky white shoes on his feet like a villain from a Bond film. The man's demeanour was also suspicious. Sometimes he surveyed the train cabin by twisting his neck in a strange manner. He was covertly looking round the whole cabin as if to see if someone was following him.

He kept on opening and closing the brown briefcase on his lap, bringing his head close to the briefcase and writing something on post-it notes. He frequently crossed off what he scribbled and wrote again. He put some of the shredded pieces of paper in his briefcase and blew some out of the window. He took out a tablet from his briefcase, jotted down some numbers from websites he was browsing, and circled them with a pencil for a long time, hiding it from the passengers in the vicinity. Then he suddenly put the tablet back in the briefcase. He turned his head in the opposite direction and shook his head. He kept on touching his waist from time to time to feel something. Terence thought, *Is there a revolver tucked in his waist?* He quickly gestured to The Secret Society of the Unwanted to meet near the toilets.

Once they were near the toilets, Terence told the gang, "That man sitting opposite me is dangerous!" Adam seemed unconvinced and asked him the reasoning behind his conclusion. He reiterated, "I have been watching him since he boarded the train. He must be planning a bank heist or something more sinister. What kind of plans were scrapped on crumpled paper!"

Adam laughed and said, "The man is a stockbroker, a middleman buying and selling shares. Name, Captain Malthe Jensen. He is Danish. He had been sitting for so long calculating the shares."

Terence asked quizzically, "How do you know all that?"

"I got the name from the side of his briefcase. I am half Danish; my mum's surname was Jensen before her marriage." He continued, "And I understood he was a stockbroker as he was browsing shares on his tablet like a pro."

Terence said with a startled face, "But did you see the way he looks?"

"If you are not a philosopher, do you have to be a bad person? He is not a bad man at all. I can say, unfortunate."

"Why?"

"It is sweltering hot outside, but his body is completely covered. He has an artificial leg. He lost balance thrice while walking. Probably he was in a major accident. That cut on the cheek is a reminder of that accident. There must be many more such spots on his body. He wears a full collared shirt to cover them. He also lost an eye in the accident. Right eye. Because if you can see through one eye only, you must wrap and twist your neck a lot. He also has a waist injury, still uses a belt. The gentleman could not sit comfortably because his belt was hurting." Adam's smile widened. "Did you understand everything, my wannabe detective friend?"

Terence felt like his soul was crushed. The mystery that he was trying to conjure up in his mind actually amounted to nothing.

He sheepishly said, "What about my desire to be you guys' assistant?"

Adam fondly reached out and stroked Terence's hair. "It is okay to be so observant, but do not judge anything at face value. A good detective never reaches a conclusion without looking beyond what a common person sees."

The children went back to their seats. Once they reached Canberra station, they boarded a pre-arranged hotel bus in an orderly manner. All the excursions were planned and timed to the second with military precision by Mr Westman. They were staying at the Leumeah Lodge for their five-day trip. The rooms were clean, and after they unpacked, the children joined the teachers for a quick fifteen-minute lunch. The children were so famished that most of them finished the delicious three slices of margherita pizza in less than ten minutes.

They all boarded the bus again and visited the Cockington Green and National Dinosaur Museum. They had dinner at six p.m. at Hogs Breath before returning to the hotel.

The next three days were exciting but uneventful. They visited the Parliament House, Australian War Memorial, had lunch at Poppy's at the War Memorial, High Court, Museum of Australian Democracy, The Royal Australian Mint, National Zoo & Aquarium and Australian Institute of Sport.

On day four, they were supposed to spend the day at the snowfields (Perisher, Selwyn, or Thredbo), but in the morning, just before breakfast, Mr Westman called the four detective friends aside for a chat. Though he had forbidden the children to do any detective work at the school, he seemed to have a change of heart after the children were felicitated for catching Mr Bond.

He told them, "Look, this may not be remarkably interesting to you, but I have a small case for you to solve. You can always say no and go ahead with the excursion with the rest of your classmates, if you do not find it interesting enough. I got a phone call from my friend, Oscar Neville. He is the descendant of the Earl of Warwick. His dad, Duke Oliver Neville who lived in the United Kingdom, chose to remarry after Oscar's mum passed away. Oscar did not particularly have a good relationship with his new stepmother and decided to move to Australia at the age of eighteen without telling his dad where he was moving to.

"Due to his challenging work and intelligence, he completed his MBBS and attained a higher medical degree FRACP by the age of thirty. He is now the owner of a chain of private hospitals, The Rest Nook, which has branches all over Australia. After opening the first branch of the Rest Nook, he reconnected with his dad. Oliver visited Australia every year to look at Oscar's accomplishments.

"He told him that he was so honoured to be his dad. He was proud that he built his empire from scratch without any help from him. Oscar absolutely revered his dad and spent as much time as he could with Oliver taking time off from his busy schedule. They travelled together from Uluru to the outback, rainforests to pristine white sand beaches, and of course, the Great Barrier Reef. They spent time at Sydney's Harbour Bridge and Opera House. They visited Noosa, Byron Bay, Bondi Beach, Perth, and the Gold Coast.

"Oliver Neville recently passed away and left him nothing except a box of books and few pictures of his dad and him when he was a boy, which were delivered to him yesterday. Oscar's feelings were a bit hurt as his dad had quite a few properties and millions of pounds in several banks in the UK. He felt disowned and unloved by his dad till he read a letter addressed to him that came accompanying the books." Mr Westman showed them the scanned letter on his phone. It read:

'Dear Son,

When you get this letter, you will know I am in heavenly abode now. Though I did not agree completely on many matters with you, it did not mean I stopped loving you as you were my firstborn.

I am so proud of what you have achieved without any assistance from me or any of your relatives. Inside the box accompanying this letter is a **Samara to two hundred solitaires worth four hundred million Shylock demands in the closet eleven of repository of land of liberty near Gallery of Dharuk**. My blessing will always be there with you, and I hope you have a wonderful and accomplished life.

Forever yours.

Dad.'

Mr Westman said, "Oscar seems baffled by the contents of the letter and cannot understand what it means. Then I mentioned to him about you four and what astute little detectives you are. He requested me to bring you over to his house. I asked Oscar to send his car this morning, and he will show the box and its contents. He could not find anything of value in the box. Maybe you can solve the mystery. He promised a handsome reward if you can locate anything valuable in the box."

The Secret Society of the Unwanted did not need much convincing. They were tired from visiting all the important places in Canberra and wanted a rest day. Perhaps this was the perfect opportunity to spend the day doing something they love, solving crimes.

A big black stretch limousine arrived at eight a.m. to take the children and Mr Westman to Dr Oscar Neville's house. As they drove into the long driveway of palatial house at the heart of Canberra, they were greeted by a suited gentleman, who showed them to the study. Within two minutes, a young, very handsome man walked into the room. Mr Westman stood up and gave a hug to the man.

He introduced the man as his friend from university, Dr Oscar Neville. Dr Neville gave them a brief summary of the background of the box, which was similar to what Mr Westman mentioned earlier. He unbolted one of the cabinets to take out a beautiful ornate box. He unlocked the box and slowly took out the contents and left them on the table. They looked like ordinary books and few framed pictures.

Harley asked Dr Neville and Mr Westman whether they could be left alone for a few hours with the box as they needed time to investigate. Dr Neville smiled and asked Mr Westman to accompany him to the lounge.

Harley, an avid book reader, said, "Okay, before we start looking into the box, we should solve the riddle."

Melissa asked, "What do you mean?"

Harley said, "We have to first solve the riddle, 'Samara to two hundred solitaires worth four hundred million Shylock demands in the closet eleven of repository of land of liberty near Gallery of Dharuk'. We know that Shylock demanded a pound of flesh. So, whatever we find is worth four hundred million pounds, which is roughly eight hundred million Australian dollars. Also, closet could mean safe or vault, repository means Bank and land of liberty is America." Adam, Melissa, and Kai's eyes lit up with excitement.

Adam shouted, "My mum has a solitaire diamond wedding ring. So, there are two hundred diamonds worth eight hundred million dollars in Safe 11 in Bank of America. We need to solve the rest to continue. Kai, can you please take out your iPad?"

Kai took out his iPad and the children started looking for synonyms of Samara, Gallery and Dharuk. One synonym of Samara was key. So, it was evident to them they had to look for a key to the safe in Bank of America in the box. Gallery could mean Museum and Dharuk meant an aboriginal language spoken in and around Sydney. So, they were looking for Bank of America near the Museum of Sydney.

Kai jumped in joy and said, "Wow, there is a Bank of America near the corner of Museum of Sydney. All we now need to find is the key in the box."

There was a knock at the door. The suited man came in with a butler with lots of snacks and drinks. After a snack break, the children started taking out each of the items in the box meticulously. They suspected that the key could be tucked in one of the four photographs frames. So, they carefully dismantled the frames, but they had no luck. There were six hard-cover books, eight soft-cover books, and four paperbacks.

They easily eliminated the eight soft-cover books and four paperbacks as they felt each of them individually and there was nothing inside. Then they looked through the pages inside the hard-cover books but no luck. Suddenly, Kai shouted, "Guys, in the book that I am holding, the inside pages are two different shades of white. Maybe it has been tampered with."

Harley, Adam, and Melissa gathered around as Kai started peeling the inside covers of the book. Tucked inside the front cover was a key covered in cellophane paper. The children shouted in unison, "Hooray!"

Oscar and Mr Westman heard the children shouting and came running into the room. Melissa told Oscar that they have found the key to Safe 11 Bank of America located near Museum of Sydney and, inside the safe, Oscar should find two hundred diamonds worth $800 million. Oscar could not believe that and cried in joy. He folded his hand and looked towards the sky, as if to ask forgiveness from his father for not being in contact more frequently and misjudging him for thinking that he disinherited him in his will.

Mr Westman was staring in awe at the kids and said that he misjudged them. They were absolutely fabulous and possessed daunting investigating skills. Oscar asked them to keep quiet about their find. He said that he would take the next available flight to Sydney to see if the key worked and he would be in touch. Mr Westman and the children had the limo for the rest of the day. They went to Sky Zone trampolining and ice-skating. They also had a scrumptious dinner at the exclusive Commonwealth Club, all paid by Oscar to thank them for their assistance.

Their classmates were looking in amazement when they arrived back to the hotel in a limo. They started asking all sorts of questions, but they had to keep mum. The next day, they checked out of the hotel and kept all the luggage in the tour bus. They visited the Canberra Deep Space Centre and National Museum of Australia before catching the train at twelve p.m. Once they boarded the train, Mr Westman's phone started ringing, and he walked away to take the phone call. He seemed incredibly happy and scribbled something on a piece of paper and handed it over to Adam.

Oscar found the diamonds in the locker of Bank of America. He was super grateful and would meet them when they were back in Sydney. The children were overjoyed and hugged each other. True to his word, Oscar was waiting for them at the train station. He handed over an envelope each to all the four children and thanked them immensely for their service.

He said that with the money he would start a charitable section in each of his private hospitals to look after underprivileged people. Also, he would change the name of his private hospitals to the Oliver Neville Foundation to honour his dad. He also handed a cheque to Mr Westman to donate towards the school fund.

Once home, the children opened the envelopes and there were thank you notes and cheques for $10,000 each towards their college funds and also an additional $20,000 to purchase detective equipment. Mr Westman said that Oscar was very generous and gave him $100,000, and he would use the money to increase the size of their school swimming pool.

The investigator quads did a teleconference with William the Wizard. He applauded them for solving the case without his help and also without using any of their magical powers. Adam asked what they should purchase to help him with their detective work.

William suggested they should get some excellent quality binoculars, a camera, evidence collection bags, notebooks, a magnifying glass, G.P.S. or a proper satellite navigational system, recording equipment, and if they did not already have them, phones, and computers. They were elated at the prospect of shopping for their new gears.

As Oscar held the letter of his late father, he knew his life would never be the same again. For now, though, he needed to find a way to live with his memories. He missed his father's sense of humour, his touch, the love they once shared, and his wisdom.